To Leela and all her aunties, especially Auntie Diki,
Auntie Suni, Auntie Lyla, and Auntie Teresa.
And to the chosen families that strengthen us.

VIKING
An imprint of Penguin Random House LLC, New York

First published in the United States of America by Viking,
an imprint of Penguin Random House LLC, 2021

Visit us online at penguinrandomhouse.com.

Library of Congress Cataloging-in-Publication Data is available.

Manufactured in China

ISBN 9780593205068

1 3 5 7 9 10 8 6 4 2

HH

Design by Opal Roengchai
Text set in Nidhi Chanani

The illustrations were created digitally
with handmade texture brushes.

WHAT WILL MY STORY BE?

NIDHI CHANANI

VIKING

I listen to my aunties tell their stories.

Their stories are bridges, strong.
Their voices like tea, steeped in love and lore.

They traveled through lands

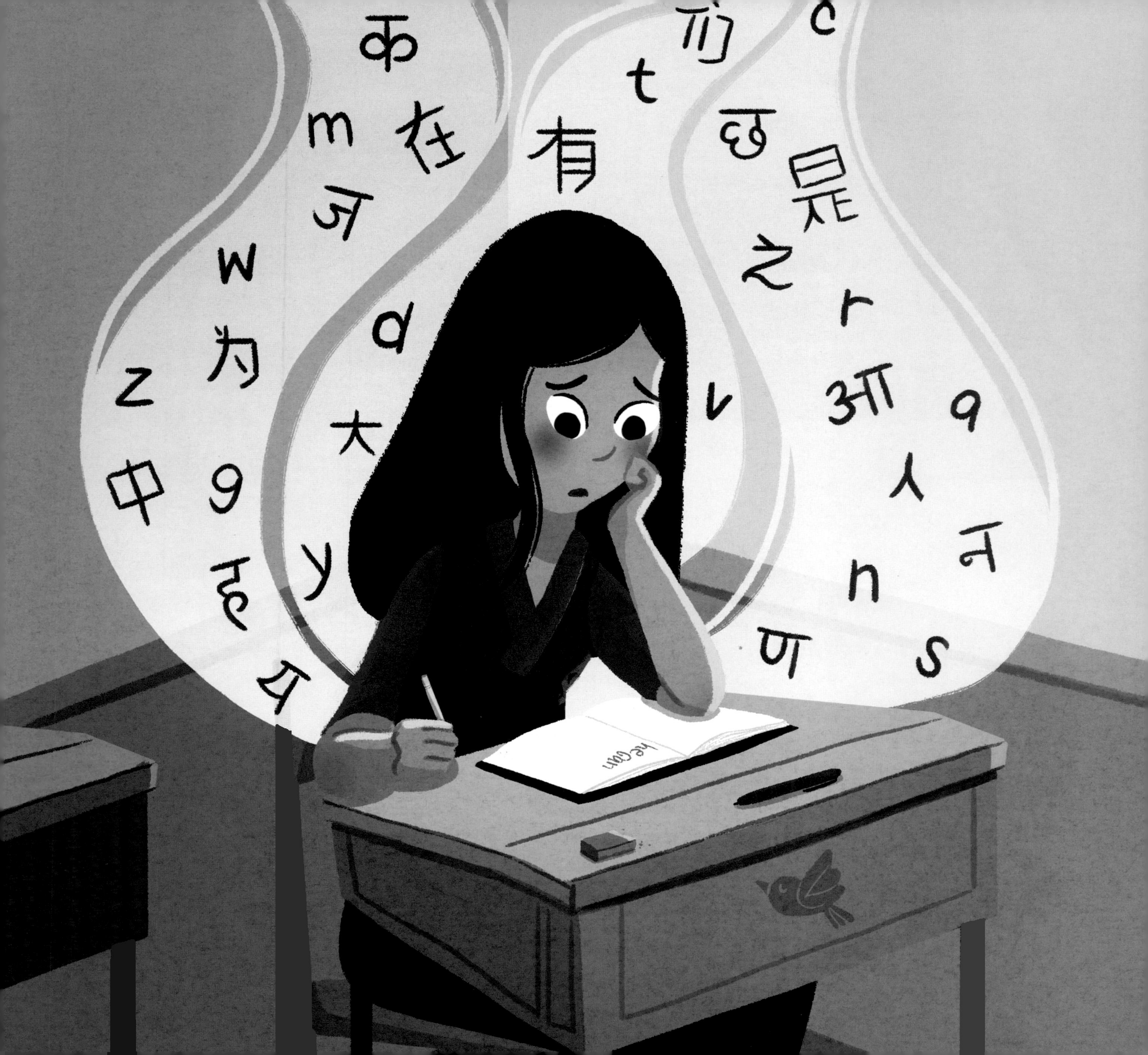

trained their tongues
to speak two, three
new languages.

I eat cake.
He eats cake.
She eats cake.
They eat cake.

Rose like waves in an ocean.

With them, I am silent.
I want to catch each word.

I want to tell my own
but what will my story be?

In my quiet, it begins.

It's slow to start,
my voice, my art.

Will I lead a ship of pantless pirates
across hundreds of islands?
Sing songs to calm the sea?

Or I could teach long-haired dragons to speak.
Would they stumble, stutter?
I would help with laughter and glee.

Maybe I will explore the world
beneath the waves.
Answer the cries of creatures
jumbo to mini.

My aunties come to hear,
come to see.

They encourage my speech,
create space and support.

Once I start, I am unstoppable.
Then I see:
My story is not one
but two, three through . . . infinity.
They are echoes calling.
They are my history.

My aunties listen to my stories
and together, our words breathe.